P9-DEK-528

BASED ON THE ORIGINAL CHARACTERS CREATED BY

JIM DAVIS

NEW YORK

GRAPHIC NOVELS AVAILABLE FROM PAPERCUTZ™

GRAPHIC NOVEL #1
"FISH TO FRY"

GRAPHIC NOVEL #2
"THE CURSE OF
THE CAT PEOPLE"

COMING SOON:

GRAPHIC NOVEL #3
"CATZILLA"

GRAPHIC NOVEL #4
"CAROLING CAPERS"

GARFIELD & Co GRAPHIC NOVELS ARE AVAILABLE IN HARDCOVER ONLY FOR $7.99 EACH. PLEASE ADD $4.00 FOR POSTAGE AND HANDLING FOR THE FIRST BOOK, ADD $1.00 FOR EACH ADDITIONAL BOOK.

PLEASE MAKE CHECK PAYABLE TO:
NBM PUBLISHING

SEND TO:
PAPERCUTZ, 1200 COUNTY RD. RTE. 523
FLEMINGTON, NJ 08822 (1-800-886-1223)

WWW.PAPERCUTZ.COM

JANICE CHIANG – LETTERING
ADAM GRANO – PRODUCTION
MICHAEL PETRANEK – ASSOCIATE EDITOR
JIM SALICRUP
EDITOR-IN-CHIEF

ISBN: 978-1-59707-266-3

PRINTED IN CHINA
FEBRUARY 2011 BY O.G. PRINTING PRODUCTIONS, LTD.
UNITS 2 & 3, 5/F, LEMMI CENTRE
50 HOI YUEN ROAD
KWON TONG, KOWLOON

DISTRIBUTED BY MACMILLAN
FIRST PAPERCUTZ PRINTING

OH, JON! YOU SHOULDN'T HAVE!

YOU MUST HAVE BETTER THINGS TO SPEND YOUR MONEY ON.

YOU ALL LOOK SO PRETTY IN THIS PICTURE.
IT MUST HAVE TAKEN YOU HOURS TO GET THIS POSE RIGHT!
NAH. IT WAS A PIECE OF CAKE!
HA!

DON'T BELIEVE THAT MAN.
YOU HAVE NO IDEA WHAT IT TOOK TO GET THAT PICTURE...

"IT ALL STARTED YESTERDAY MORNING...
"IT HAD BEEN A PERFECT DAY.
"WOKE UP AT TEN, HAD BREAKFAST, BACK IN BED BY 10:15.
YAWN! ALMOST TIME FOR MY PRE-LUNCH SNACK...
GARFIELD, ODIE... THIS IS VERY IMPORTANT!
MORE IMPORTANT THAN EATING AND SLEEPING?

TOMORROW IS LIZ'S BIRTHDAY.
NOT VERY IMPORTANT.
AND WE ARE GOING TO GIVE HER A VERY SPECIAL GIFT! A FAMILY PHOTO!
SUPER...

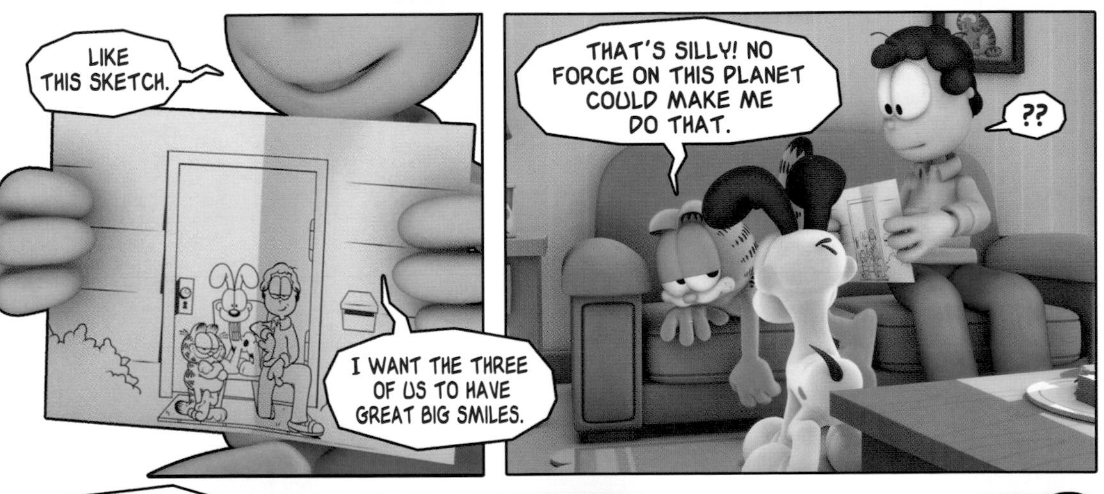
LIKE THIS SKETCH.
I WANT THE THREE OF US TO HAVE GREAT BIG SMILES.
THAT'S SILLY! NO FORCE ON THIS PLANET COULD MAKE ME DO THAT.
??

AND IF YOU GUYS CO-OPERATE AND WE GET THE PICTURE EXACTLY RIGHT, THERE'LL BE EXTRA LASAGNA TONIGHT.

OKAY! I'M IN!

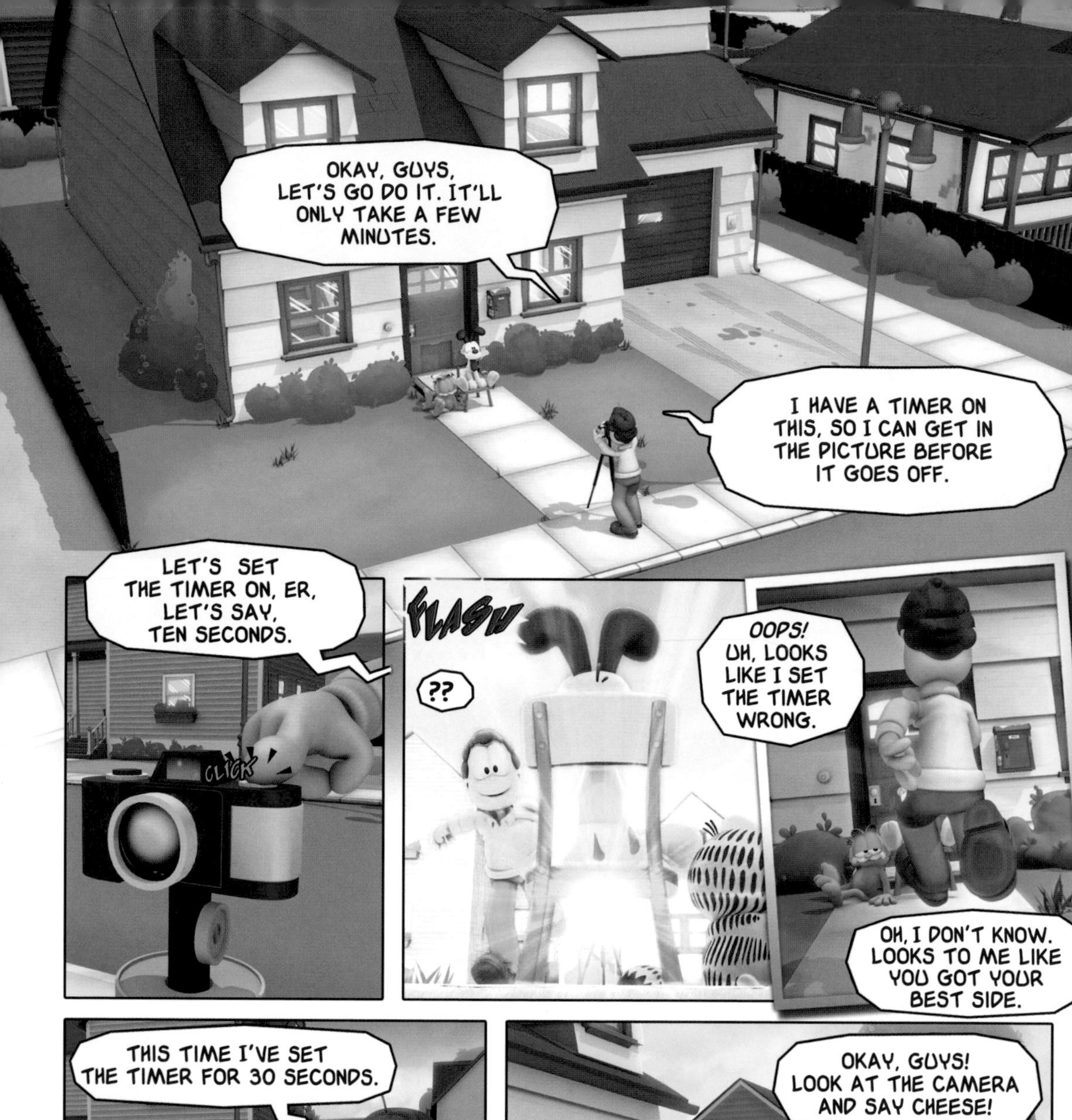
OKAY, GUYS, LET'S GO DO IT. IT'LL ONLY TAKE A FEW MINUTES.
I HAVE A TIMER ON THIS, SO I CAN GET IN THE PICTURE BEFORE IT GOES OFF.
LET'S SET THE TIMER ON, ER, LET'S SAY, TEN SECONDS.
CLICK
FLASH
??
OOPS! UH, LOOKS LIKE I SET THE TIMER WRONG.
OH, I DON'T KNOW. LOOKS TO ME LIKE YOU GOT YOUR BEST SIDE.

THIS TIME I'VE SET THE TIMER FOR 30 SECONDS.

OKAY, GUYS! LOOK AT THE CAMERA AND SAY CHEESE!

CHEESE!

HURRY UP! I'VE GOT A CRAMP IN MY JAW!

MAYBE I FORGOT TO PUSH THE RIGHT BUTTON.
...

SAY CHEESE!

BONK
FLAP
FLAP

FLASH

MAYBE ONE WITH NERMAL?

MEOW!

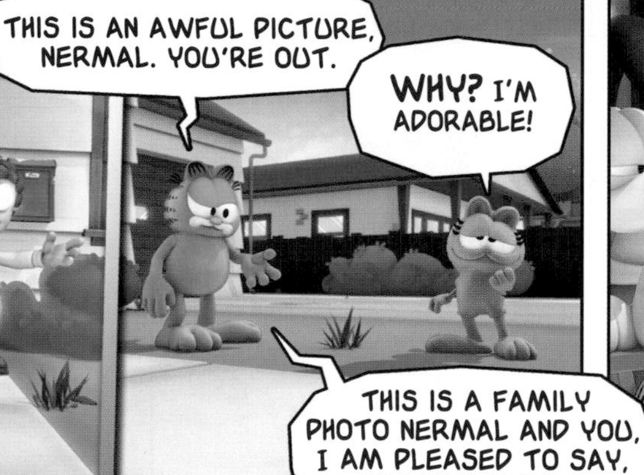
THIS IS AN AWFUL PICTURE, NERMAL. YOU'RE OUT.
WHY? I'M ADORABLE!
THIS IS A FAMILY PHOTO NERMAL AND YOU, I AM PLEASED TO SAY, ARE NOT FAMILY.

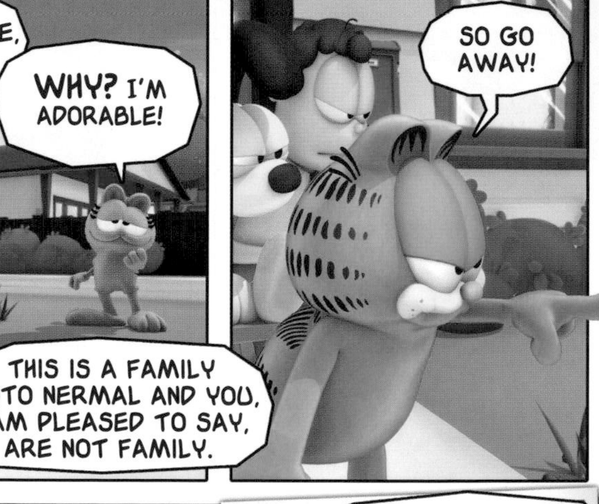
SO GO AWAY!

HI, NEIGHBOR.

I'VE RUN OUT OF SUGAR. CAN I BORROW SOME FROM YOU?

WELL DONE, JON, GOOD SHOT OF THE NEIGHBOR.

"AND SO IT WENT ON ALL DAY...
COUGH
COUGH
COUGH
VROOOOMM
ODIE, STOP! NAUGHTY DOG!
FLASH
OOPS!
HELLO? YES, ERR...
FLASH
MEOW!
NERMAL, NO!
BLAST! MY NOSE IS ITCHING.
HOW'S THE FAMILY PHOTO COMING ALONG?
AAHH! A WASP!
FLASH
AND THE WEATHER FORECAST WAS FOR CLEAR SKIES...

THIS IS IT!
SAY CHEESE!

SOMEONE ORDER
A LARGE PIZZA WITH
EXTRA PEPPERONI?
YES!

GARFIELD!

NOOOOOOOOOOOOOOOOOO!

IT'S YOUR FAULT.
YOU'VE MADE ME
THINK ABOUT PIZZA
ALL DAY.

I'VE HAD
ENOUGH.
IT'S TIME TO DO
SOMETHING DRASTIC.

OKAY! EVERYONE READY?
DO YOU THINK THIS LOOKS OKAY?

OF COURSE!
I AM A PROFESSIONAL PHOTOGRAPHER! I CAN EVEN MAKE YOU LOOK GOOD!
IF YOU'D DONE THIS IN THE FIRST PLACE, IT WOULD HAVE SAVED US A LOT OF GRIEF!

DON'T MOVE! ONE, TWO, THREE... CHEESE!!!
I NEED MORE PIZZA.

FLASH
FLASH
FLASH
FLASH

FLASH
FLASH
FLASH
MAGNIFICENT! I HAVE OUTDONE MYSELF.

I SHALL MAKE A PRINT FOR YOUR LADY FRIEND.
WHEW.

AND THAT'S WHAT IT TOOK TO GET THE PICTURE FOR LIZ'S BIRTHDAY...

WELL, IT'S A GREAT PHOTO AND I THANK YOU ALL FOR IT...

IT'S JUST...
SOMETHING WRONG WITH IT?

OH, NO, IT'S GREAT. BUT...
...WELL, THERE'S A CERTAIN EXPRESSION I KNOW YOU FOR... A SPECIAL LOOK...
?

WHAT LOOK IS THAT?

OH!

THAT'S IT, JON! THAT'S THE LOOK I KNOW YOU FOR.
YAARG!

I KNOW THAT LOOK VERY WELL...

THE END

GARFIELD
& Co
NICE TO NERMAL
GRRRRRR! CAN'T SLEEP EITHER, POOKY?
DON'T WORRY. I'LL TAKE CARE OF IT.

??
CLICK

OH! GARFIELD! I'M TRYING TO CLEAN!

JON! I'M TRYING TO SLEEP.

I'LL VACUUM LATER. I'LL DO THE LAUNDRY NOW.

PEACE AT LAST.

HIYA, GARFIELD!

I'VE COME TO SPEND THE DAY WITH YOU.
ARE YOU GLAD TO SEE ME?
NERMAL.

HASTA LA VISTA!
KICK
HELP!

BETTER DO GARFIELD'S BLANKET WHILE I'M AT IT.
PIZZ

POOKY, YOU STAY HERE.

I WONDER WHAT KIND OF BLEACH IS GOOD FOR LASAGNA STAINS.

THAT WASN'T VERY NICE!
YOU KNOW, YOU SHOULD HAVE A PLACE IN YOUR HOME FOR GUESTS LIKE ME!

??
WE DO.

THE PERFECT PLACE.

HE'LL BE SORRY!
ONE OF THESE DAYS, GARFIELD IS GOING TO BE NICE TO ME!
WOW. AND I THINK TODAY'S THE DAY.

I'VE WASHED THE BLANKET IN YOUR BED, GARFIELD.
SNIFF!

BUT NOW IT DOESN'T SMELL LIKE LASAGNA. OH, WELL. GUESS I'LL JUST HAVE TO SPILL SOME MORE.

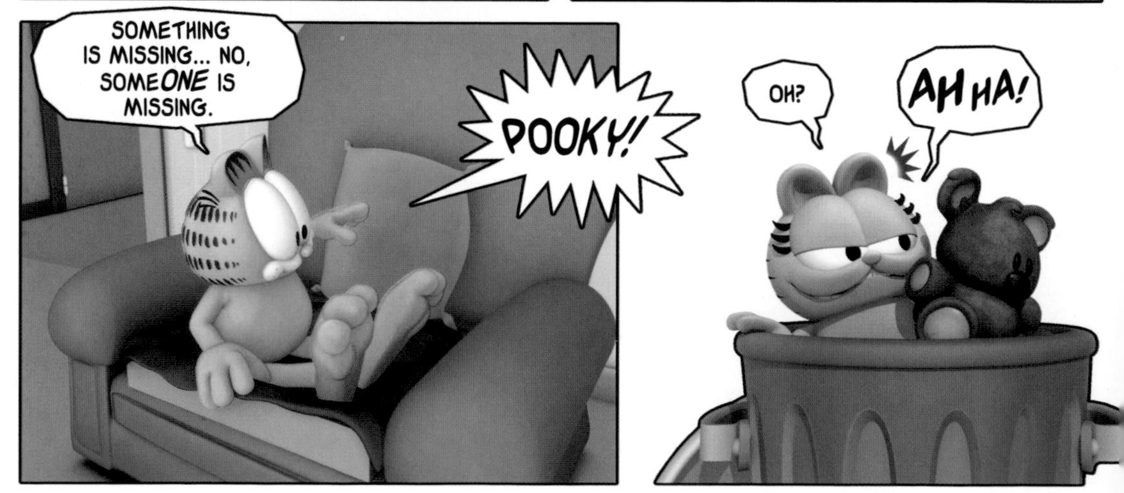
SOMETHING IS MISSING... NO, SOMEONE IS MISSING.
POOKY!
OH?
AH HA!

OH, POOKY! WHERE ARE YOU?
OH, WELL. HE'LL TURN UP. IT'S NOT LIKE I CAN'T LIVE WITHOUT HIM FOR TWO MINUTES.
YES, IT IS! POOKY! POOKY, WHERE ARE YOU?
POOKY, ARE YOU IN HERE?
SO THAT'S WHAT HAPPENED TO MY CORNED BEEF SANDWICH.
I'VE BEEN AT IT SINCE 6 AM BUT MY SPRING CLEANING IS ALL DONE, LIZ.
GASP!
WHAT? I... I... BUT I JUST...
I'LL CALL YOU BACK, LIZ.

POOKY!
COME OUT, COME OUT WHEREVER YOU ARE!

GARF!
HAND HIM OVER, ARBUCKLE, IF YOU KNOW WHAT'S GOOD FOR YOU.
PIZZA

I TOOK POOKY OUT OF YOUR BED SO I COULD WASH THE BLANKET...
...AND I PUT POOKY RIGHT HERE ON THE...

OH!
I MUST HAVE ACCIDENTALLY KNOCKED HIM INTO THE WASTE-BASKET. BUT THEN I EMPTIED IT INTO THE TRASH CANS OUTSIDE.

DON'T WORRY, POOKY, I'M COMING TO SAVE YOU!

POOKY? WHERE ARE YOU, POOKY?
THERE'S NO POOKY IN THERE.
I CAN'T BELIEVE I'LL NEVER SEE MY LITTLE POOKY AGAIN. NEVER SEE HIS SMILING FACE. NEVER HEAR HIS FRIENDLY VOICE.
OKAY, HE DOESN'T SAY MUCH BUT HE WAS MY PAL...

WHO COULD BE SO THOROUGHLY ROTTEN AS TO TAKE MY BELOVED POOKY?
ME!
HEE HEE HEE!

YOU DIDN'T.
I DID. FOUND HIM IN THE TRASH, RIGHT WHERE YOU DUMPED ME.

YOU GIVE ME BACK MY POOKY...
...OR I'LL MAIL YOU TO ABU DHABI IN A BOX MARKED PLEASE BEND, FOLD, AND MUTILATE!
YOU LAY ONE PAW ON ME, GARFIELD, AND YOU'LL NEVER SEE POOKY AGAIN!

YOU CAN HAVE HIM BACK ON ONE CONDITION...
YOU HAVE TO BE NICE TO ME!

YOU WOULDN'T SETTLE FOR ALMOST NICE?
OH, YOU WIN.
DEAL! BUT YOU HAVE TO BE NICE TO ME ALL DAY.

BEING NICE TO NERMAL. IT'S UNNATURAL! I NEED A COOKIE. OR TWO.
...OR THIRTY-SEVEN.

??!
WHO'S EATEN ALL THE COOKIES?

ODIE, NERMAL IS IN MY BED WITH HIS STOMACH FULL OF MY COOKIES...

...AND I CAN'T DO ANYTHING ABOUT IT.

YOU KNOW, GARFIELD, I TRULY AM THE CUTEST KITTY CAT IN THE WHOLE WORLD. DON'T YOU AGREE?
SAY IT!

YES, NERMAL... YOU ARE THE CUTEST KITTY CAT.

I DIDN'T HEAR YOU. SAY IT AGAIN.
...

YOU ARE THE CUTEST KITTY CAT IN THE WHOLE WORLD.

THANK YOU.
WILL YOU LET ME HAVE ALL YOUR LASAGNA TONIGHT?

I CAN'T TAKE ANY MORE.
I DIDN'T WANT TO DO IT, NOT EVEN TO NERMAL. BUT I HAVE TO.

I'M INVITING JON'S COUSINS, DRUSILLA AND MINERVA, TO COME AND VISIT!

THERE... SENT!

DING DONG
?

HI, COUSIN JON! WE CAME TO VISIT!

OH, LOOK! THERE'S A CUTE KITTY! HELLO LITTLE KITTY CAT!

HE'S THE CUTEST KITTY I'VE EVER SEEN. BUT HE COULD BE EVEN CUTER!
?

GARFIELD! YOU'VE GOT TO SAVE ME FROM THEM!
YOU PROMISED TO BE NICE TO ME!

I'M BEING NICE TO YOU. THEY'RE THE ONES WHO AREN'T BEING NICE TO YOU.

GEE, I'D HELP YOU, NERMAL, BUT I HAVEN'T BEEN MYSELF SINCE POOKY DISAPPEARED.
HE'S IN THE HOLLOW TREE IN THE BACK YARD!

POOKY! THERE YOU ARE, MY FRIEND!

I'LL HELP NERMAL AFTER POOKY AND I GET REACQUAINTED.

DON'T BOTHER.

WELL, ODIE... I'VE GOT POOKY BACK AND I NEVER HAVE TO BE NICE TO NERMAL AGAIN.
EVERYTHING WORKED OUT FINE.
THERE'S ANOTHER CUTE KITTY!
OH, NO!
LET ME GO! NO! SAVE ME!
WE'LL CURL HIS FUR!
THE END

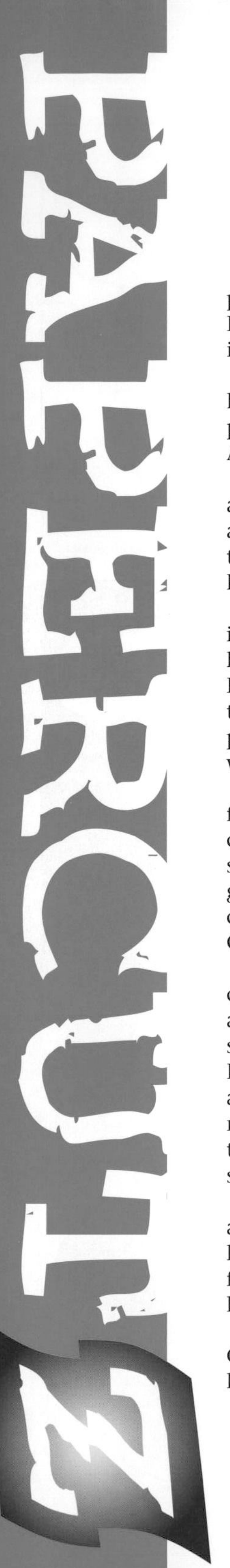

WATCH OUT FOR PAPERCUTZ™

Welcome to the first GARFIELD graphic novel from Papercutz, the little publisher with the biggest stars. I'm Jim Salicrup, the Editor-in-Chief at Papercutz, but in the world of Garfield, the really important guy named Jim is Jim Davis, the creator of Garfield.

Jim Davis was born July 28, 1945 and was promptly dropped on his head, which would explain his life-long desire to sit around and draw silly pictures. His parents, Jim and Betty Davis, were farmers who raised Black Angus cows and feed crops for the cattle… not to mention 25 cats.

Jim and his little brother, Davey, grew up with a lot of responsibilities and chores, and lots of cats. When Jim was just a little boy he developed asthma — a breathing problem brought on by allergies (probably due to all the hay on the farm). Asthma makes you cough, hack, and wheeze, and Jim had to stay indoors a lot.

One day, when Jim's mom noticed he was bored, she shoved a pencil in his hand and gave him a stack of paper and told him to draw to "keep himself entertained." And he did. One of his first drawings was a cow. Because it was hardly recognizable, Jim labeled it "cow." Next, he discovered that drawings were funnier if they had words. Before long, Jim had gotten pretty good at drawing. He couldn't stop! He drew on tables. He drew on walls. He even drew on the cattle!

Years later, Jim turned his attention to the comics pages and tried to figure out what was working and why. There were lots of dogs on the comics pages — Snoopy, Marmaduke, Belvedere — but no cats! Jim began sketching cats, drawing on his childhood memories of the 25 farm cats he grew up with. The cat that struck him as the funniest was a big fat grouchy character that he named Garfield after his opinionated grandfather, James Garfield Davis.

At first, Garfield was simply the sidekick to the star of the strip — a cartoonist named Jon Arbuckle. But Jim quickly realized that Garfield had all the funny lines. A star was born. On June 19, 1978, Garfield the comic strip made its first appearance in 41 US newspapers in cities including Boston, Dallas, and Chicago. By 1987 the strip was in 2,000 newspapers, and today, the strip is in almost every newspaper in the world. Over 2,600 newspapers now carry Garfield and an estimated 263,000,000 people read the strip every day. In fact, the strip is the most widely syndicated comic strip in the world, according to Guinness World Records.

So, are we thrilled at Papercutz to be able to publish comics based on the animated Garfield TV series seen on Cartoon Network? Does Garfield love lasagna? At Papercutz we're dedicated to producing great graphic novels for all ages, and we're proud and honored to add GARFIELD & Co to our line-up.

Also at booksellers everywhere: GARFIELD & Co #2 "The Curse of the Cat People" — with three more misadventures of our favorite lasagna-loving cat. Don't miss it!

Till then, watch out for Papercutz!

Jim

(Salicrup, not Davis)

GARFIELD
& Co
FISH TO FRY
...AND THE HALIBUT IS THE LARGEST OF THE FLATFISH, FOUND IN BOTH THE NORTH PACIFIC AND THE NORTH ATLANTIC OCEANS...
FISH! BEAUTIFUL, DELICIOUS FISH.
HALIBUT CAN GROW AS LARGE AS NINE HUNDRED POUNDS LIKE THIS ONE.
GET ME THAT FISH! GET ME THAT FISH AND AN EQUAL WEIGHT OF FRENCH FRIES.
RING RING
OH. HI, LIZ.
YOUR FISH? ...IN THIS HOUSE? ...LOOK AFTER THEM...
...WHILE YOU'RE AWAY?
FISH?
DID HE SAY FISH?
I DON'T THINK THAT WOULD BE SUCH A GOOD IDEA...
...GARFIELD HEARD ME.
OKAY, I'LL KEEP HIM AWAY FROM THEM.

GARFIELD! LIZ IS LEAVING HER PET FISH HERE WHILE SHE'S OUT OF TOWN. YOU WILL LEAVE THEM ALONE OR ELSE...

HAVE NO FEAR, ARBUCKLE. I WON'T EAT LIZ'S FISH.
TRUST ME.

ONE FISH, TWO FISH, THREE FISH...
ZZZZZ

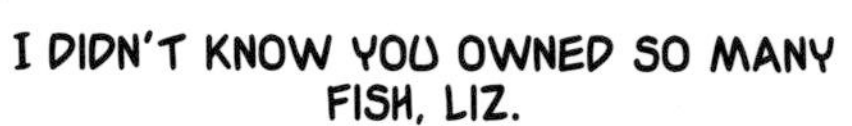
I DIDN'T KNOW YOU OWNED SO MANY FISH, LIZ.

??
SMELLS LIKE FISH...

WOW!!!

THAT IS THE MOST BEAUTIFUL...

...BUFFET...

...I'VE EVER SEEN IN MY LIFE!

YOU'LL DO FOR A START.

??

HELP ME!

PTOOIE

THAT WAS A PUFFER FISH!

HMMM. YOU LOOK VERY TASTY!

AAAPPP
ZZZ

AAAH!
BRAZILIAN ELECTRIC DANCING FISH LIKE AN ELECTRIC EEL!

NOW! YOUR TURN MY BEAUTY!

MMMMM! HE WASN'T BAD. LET'S SEE WHAT HE IS...

??

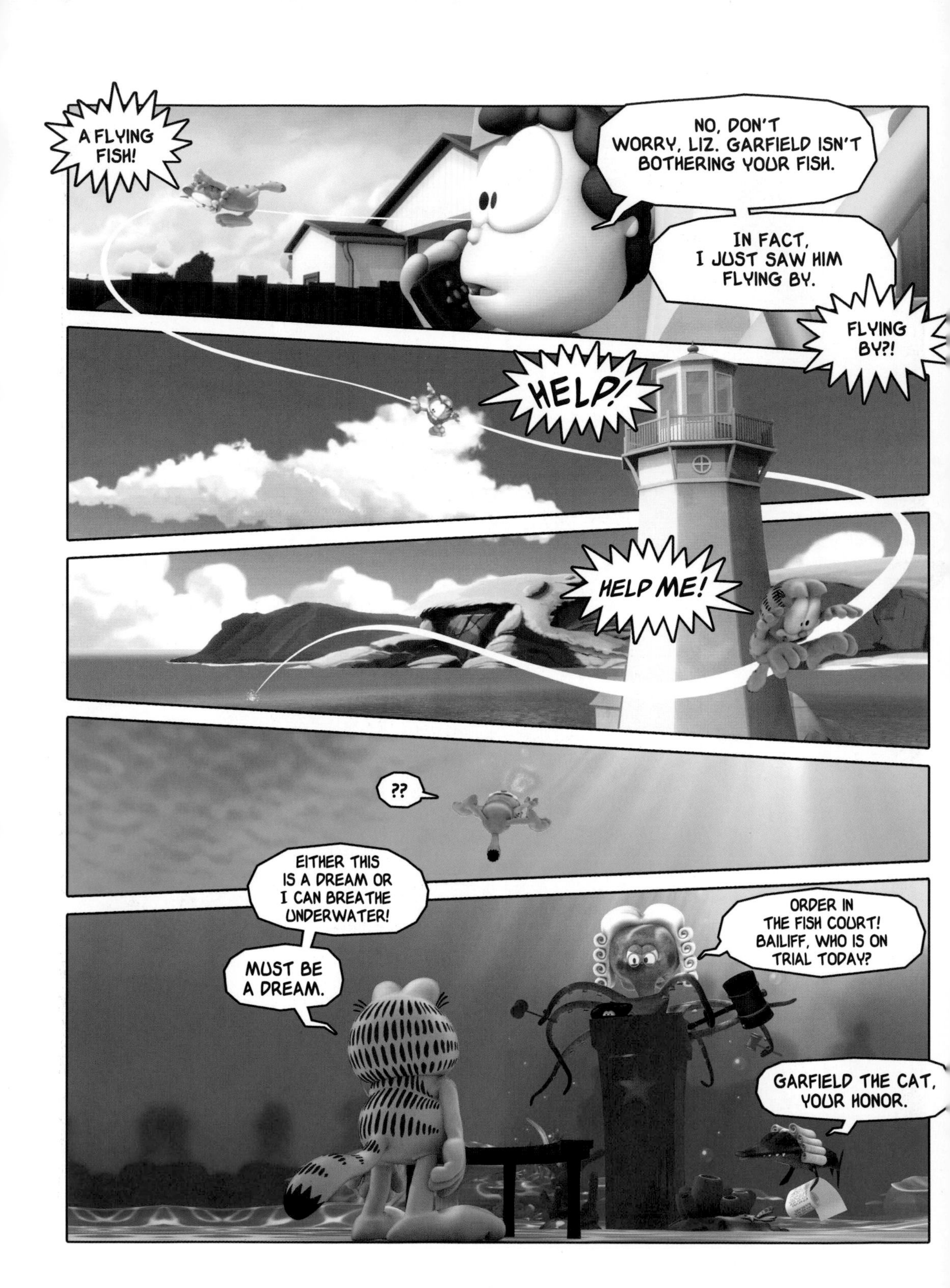
A FLYING FISH!
NO, DON'T WORRY, LIZ. GARFIELD ISN'T BOTHERING YOUR FISH.
IN FACT, I JUST SAW HIM FLYING BY.
FLYING BY?!
HELP!
HELP ME!
??
EITHER THIS IS A DREAM OR I CAN BREATHE UNDERWATER!
MUST BE A DREAM.
ORDER IN THE FISH COURT! BAILIFF, WHO IS ON TRIAL TODAY?
GARFIELD THE CAT, YOUR HONOR.

GARFIELD THE CAT IS ACCUSED OF EATING FISH.

WELL, MAYBE I ATE A FEW FISH...
7,322! TO BE EXACT, YOUR HONOR.

I'VE HEARD ENOUGH!

JURY, WHAT IS YOUR VERDICT?
GUILTY!

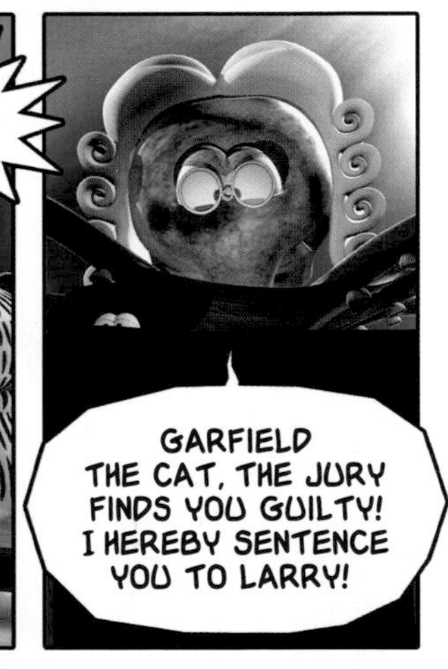
GARFIELD THE CAT, THE JURY FINDS YOU GUILTY! I HEREBY SENTENCE YOU TO LARRY!

??

HELP!
HEY, IT REALLY WAS A DREAM.

I'VE BROUGHT MY FISH AS WE DISCUSSED.
??
DON'T WORRY, GARFIELD WON'T BOTHER THEM.

SHE ONLY HAS TWO GOLDFISH. HA!
WELL, IT'S TIME FOR BREAKFAST...

MMM. A TARTAR SAUCE SANDWICH.

COME ON, YOU DIDN'T THINK I'D EAT LIZ'S GOLDFISH, DID YOU? AFTER THAT DREAM I'LL NEVER EAT ANOTHER FISH AGAIN...
UNTIL NEXT WEEK!
END